The Story of The Curse

Written By Darien K. Belcher Jr.

Illustrated By Hatice Bayramoglu

Darien Belcher Jr

This book is dedicated to my parents, friends and family but mostly to Mrs. Vanessa Johnson my summer school teacher, for the past 4years, at Sunshine Academy. Thank you for being so patient and for inspiring me to write.

Join Lego Boy and his Superhero friends as they set out to remove the curse that was put on the people who were once free. The Superhero friends will work together to beat the bad guys: Powerful Paw-Paw, Slimey Boy, and Crabby Boy. Will the Superheroes remove the curse, or will the bad guys defeat them?

Characters:

Invisible Boy... Roman Belcher

Wooden Boy... Gabriel Jones

Supertwins... Mom and Dad

Electric Boy...TJ

Fire Boy... Niles

Flash... Kyron Belcher

Lego Boy... Darien Belcher

Powerful Paw-Paw... Mr. Johnson

Slimey Boy

Crabby Boy

The people had to give the witch everything they had and listen to everything she had to say or be destroyed. She wanted diamonds, gold and all the jewelry.

The evil witch put Powerful Paw-Paw, limey Boy and Crabby Boy in charge of keeping the rare stuff safe.

In the meantime...

Now You See Me

Now You Don'

The Supertwins called some of the superheroes to a
meeting. Invisible Boy and Wooden Boy came to the meeting.

They discussed how to beat the bad guys.
At the same time the bad guys were also discussing how they
were going to set a trap and capture the superheroes.

Inside the evil tower, Slimey Boy
was setting a trap to capture
Wooden Boy
and Invisible Boy.

Slimey Boy set up an
alarm and placed pressure
pads in the evil tower and
once you step on them they
launch you in the air.

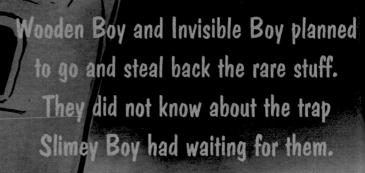

Wooden Boy and Invisible Boy planned
to go and steal back the rare stuff.
They did not know about the trap
Slimey Boy had waiting for them.

When the day came, Wooden Boy and Invisble Boy snuck into the tower.

They had gotten close to where the hidden rare stuff, jewels and diamonds were at and an alarm went off. Wooden Boy stepped on one of the pressure pads and was launched into the air. While up in the air, Wooden Boy got slimed and the trap door closed.

Invisible Boy was able to escape to tell the others about the trap. The Supertwins told Fire Boy and Invisible Boy to go back and try to free Wooden Boy from Slimey. Invisible Boy had to make Fire Boy invisible to sneak him inside of the evil tower.

Now You See Me

But once inside he became visible again. As they were walking in front of the mighty throne, Fire Boy fired a fireball at the throne and it unlocked Wooden Boy from Slimey and he was free.

Wooden Boy, Fire Boy and Invisible
Boy were running through the tower to find
the rare stuff.

Crabby Boy had set his super net in place and all of a sudden Wooden Boy and Fire Boy were trapped in Crabby's super net. Invisible Boy was able to escape again.

Invisible Boy told the Supertwins what happened.
The Supertwins were worried the superheroes were getting caught in
every trap that the bad guys set.

The people had no more rare stuff, gold or
diamonds to give. They were afraid that the
wicked witch would eventually destroy
them all.

The Supertwins knew it was time to
free the people from the curse.

In the meantime, Powerful Paw-Paw had placed a super force field around the evil tower. He planned to capture the rest of the superheroes.

Lego Boy, Electric Boy, Flash and Invisible Boy had to come up with a plan to break the powerful force field. They knew they had to save Wooden Boy and Fire Boy first before they could rescue their rare stuff, gold jewelry and diamonds.

They decided to combine their power to defeat Slimey Boy, Crabby Boy and Powerful Paw-Paw. Flash was known for his speed and ability to create powerful wind.

Now You See Me

Now You Don't

Electric Boy had 10,000 volts of power and is able to melt brick and metal. Lego Boy has many arms, he can fly and climb at great speed.

Lego Boy, Invisible Boy, Flash and Electric Boy practice
their moves and set up a plan to
blow up the force field.

When the Superheroes got to the evil tower,
the forcefield covered the entire tower.

Electric Boy, with his 10,000 volts of electricity, aimed his
electric beam at
the force field and it blew up.

Flash with his powerful speed, raced to look for Wooden Boy and Fire Boy. When he finally found them, they were still trapped in the wet super net.

Flash started spinning like a tornado until the super net dried enough so that Fire Boy could set it on fire and get free.

In the meantime, Electric Boy,
Lego Boy and Invisible Boy were looking for the
rare stuff and they met up with Crabby Boy.

Lego Boy threw Crabby Boy against the wall and knocked him out.

On the other side of the tower, Flash, Wooden Boy and Fire Boy found the rare stuff, diamonds and jewels.

Finally, the evil witch powers were weakening. Crabby Boy, Slimey and Powerful Paw-Paw gave up. They went into the real world.

The bad guys became good and joined the superheroes.
The curse was broken and the evil tower collapsed .

THE END

Hi, my name is Darien Belcher Jr. but most people call me DJ. I am 9 years old, in the 4th grade and live in Michigan. I have two brothers, Kyron and Roman. I enjoy playing video games, basketball, football, swimming, golf and singing in the youth choir at my church. I would like to be an Engineer and a Scientist when I grow up. I wrote this book in the 2nd grade and I am so excited that it is finally being published!

Join Lego Boy and his Superhero friends as they set out to remove the curse that was put on the people who were once free. The Superhero friends will work together to beat the bad guys: Powerful Paw-Paw, Slimey Boy, and Crabby Boy. Will the Superheroes remove the curse, or will the bad guys defeat them?

ISBN 978-1-7320950-6-9

$12.99

51299>

9 781732 095069